MOLLY GARRETT BANG

Wiley and the Hairy Man

ADAPTED FROM AN AMERICAN
FOLK TALE

Ready-to-Read®

ALADDIN BOOKS
Macmillan Publishing Company
New York

Collier Macmillan Publishers
London

ACKNOWLEDGMENTS

Thanks to *Swallow* and the Trailside Museum

This folk tale is based on "Wiley and the Hairy Man," as recorded by Donnell Van de Voort in "Manuscripts of the Federal Writers' Project of the Works Progress Administration for the State of Alabama" and published in *A Treasury of American Folklore*, edited by B. A. Botkin.

Aladdin Books
Macmillan Publishing Company
866 Third Avenue, New York, NY 10022
Collier Macmillan Canada, Inc.

First Aladdin Books edition 1987

Printed in the United States of America

A hardcover edition of *Wiley and the Hairy Man* is available from Macmillan Publishing Company

10   9   8   7   6   5

Library of Congress Cataloging-in-Publication Data
Bang, Molly.
Wiley and the Hairy Man.
(Ready-to-read)
Summary: With his mother's help, Wiley outwits the hairy creature that dominates the swamp near his home by the Tombigbee River.
[1. Folklore—Unites States]   I. Title.   II. Series.
[PZ8.1.B228Wi 1987]   398.2'1'0973 [E]   87-2540
ISBN 0-689-71162-X (pbk.)

FOR MY PARENTS

It was a long time ago.
Wiley and his mother
lived near a swamp.
The swamp was near
the Tombigbee River.

One day Wiley wanted

to cut some bamboo.

He needed poles for the hen roost.

He got his ax to go down to the swamp.

Wiley's mother said,
"Wiley, be careful
when you go to the swamp.
Take your hound dogs with you.
The Hairy Man will get you
if you don't watch out."

Wiley's mother knew
the Hairy Man hated hound dogs.
She knew because she knew all
about the ways of the swamp.
She had grown up on
the Tombigbee River.

Wiley said,
"I'll watch out.
I'll take my hound dogs with me
everywhere I go."

But when he got to the swamp,
his dogs saw a wild pig.
They ran after it.
They ran so far away Wiley
couldn't even hear them yelp.
"Well," thought Wiley,
"I hope the Hairy Man
isn't anywhere around here."
He took his ax
and began cutting poles.

When Wiley looked up,
there was the Hairy Man.
He was coming through the
trees. He sure was ugly.
He was hairy all over.
His eyes burned like coals.
His teeth were big
and sharp and white.
He was swinging a sack.

Wiley was scared.
Quick as he could,
he climbed up a
big bay tree.
Wiley had seen that
the Hairy Man had
feet like a cow.
And Wiley knew
a cow could not
climb a tree.

The Hairy Man stood
at the foot of the tree.
He called,
"Wiley, what are you
doing up there?"
Wiley said,
"My mother told me
to stay away from you."

Then Wiley asked,
"What's in your
big old sack?"
"Nothing yet,"
the Hairy Man said.
He picked up Wiley's ax
and began to chop down
the tree.

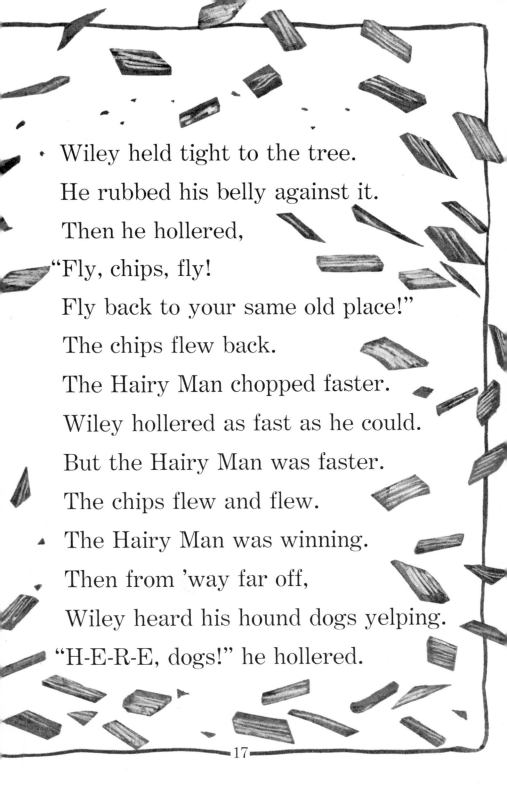

Wiley held tight to the tree.

He rubbed his belly against it.

Then he hollered,

"Fly, chips, fly!

Fly back to your same old place!"

The chips flew back.

The Hairy Man chopped faster.

Wiley hollered as fast as he could.

But the Hairy Man was faster.

The chips flew and flew.

The Hairy Man was winning.

Then from 'way far off,

Wiley heard his hound dogs yelping.

"H-E-R-E, dogs!" he hollered.

The dogs came running.

As soon as the Hairy Man saw them,

he fled away into the swamp.

When Wiley got home,
he told his mother
what had happened.
"Did the Hairy Man have his sack
with him?" she asked.
"Yes, ma'am, he did," said Wiley.

"Well," his mother said,
"the next time the Hairy Man
   comes after you, don't climb a tree.
   Just stay on the ground and say,
'Hello, Hairy Man.'
   The Hairy Man will say,
'Hello, Wiley.'

"Then you say,
'I hear you're the best
conjure man around here.'"
"What's 'conjure'?"
Wiley asked his mother.
She answered,
"It's magic."

She went on,
"You tell him he is the best
conjure man, and he'll say,
'I reckon I am.'
Then you say,
'I bet you can't
change yourself
into a giraffe.'
And he will
change himself
into a giraffe.

"Then you say,
'I bet you can't change yourself
into an alligator.'
And he will change himself
into an alligator.
You keep telling him
what he can't do.
He'll keep doing it
just to show you.

"Then you say,
'Everybody can change
into something BIG.
I bet you can't change yourself
into a little possum.'
He will change into
a little possum.
You grab him right away
and throw him into his sack.
Then you take the sack
and throw it into the river."

Wiley was scared to do
what his mother said.
But the next time he had
to go to the swamp,
he tied up his hound dogs.

As soon as he got to the swamp,

Wiley saw the Hairy Man.

He was coming at him through the trees.

He was swinging his sack.

He was grinning because he knew

Wiley had left his hound dogs behind.

Wiley wanted to run away,

but he stayed there.

He said, "Hello, Hairy Man."

And the Hairy Man said, "Hello, Wiley."

"Hairy Man," said Wiley,

"I hear you're the best

conjure man around here."

"I reckon I am," said the Hairy Man.

"I bet you can't change yourself
into a giraffe," said Wiley.
"Sure I can," the Hairy Man said.
"That's no trouble at all."
The Hairy Man twisted around,
and he changed himself into a giraffe.

Then Wiley said,
"I bet you can't change yourself
into an alligator."
The giraffe twisted around
and changed itself
into an alligator.

So Wiley said,
"Everybody can change
into something BIG.
I bet you can't change yourself
into a little possum."
The alligator twisted around
and changed itself
into a little possum.
Wiley grabbed the possum
and threw it into the
Hairy Man's sack.

He tied the sack as tight as he could.
Then he threw the sack into
the Tombigbee River.
Wiley started back home
through the swamp.
He felt happy.

But he hadn't gone far, when
there was the Hairy Man again.
He was coming at Wiley.
Wiley climbed right up the nearest tree.
"How did you get out?"
he called down to the Hairy Man.
"I changed myself into the wind,"
said the Hairy Man,
"and I blew my way out.
Now I'm going to wait right down here.
You'll get hungry,
and you'll come down
out of that tree."

Wiley thought and thought.
He thought about the
Hairy Man waiting below.
He thought about his
hound dogs tied up at home.
After a while Wiley said,
"Hairy Man, you did some
pretty good tricks.
But I bet you can't
make things disappear."
The Hairy Man said,
"Ha! That's what I'm best at.
See the bird's nest on that branch?"
Wiley looked. It was there.
Then it was gone.

But Wiley said,

"I never saw it in the first place.

I bet you can't make something

I know is there disappear."

"Look at your shirt, Wiley,"

the Hairy Man said.

Wiley looked down.

His shirt was gone!

"Oh, that was just a plain old shirt,"

he said. "But this rope

around my pants is magic.

My mother conjured it.

I bet you can't make

this rope disappear."

The Hairy Man said, "I can make all
the rope in this county disappear."
"I bet you can't," said Wiley.
The Hairy Man threw out his chest.
He opened his mouth wide
and he hollered loud,
"All the rope in this county,
DISAPPEAR!"

The rope around Wiley's pants was gone.

He held his pants up with one hand.

He held on to the tree with the other,

and he hollered loud,

"H-E-R-E, dogs!"

The dogs came running,

and the Hairy Man fled away.

When Wiley got home, he told
his mother what had happened.
"Well," she said,
"you fooled the Hairy Man twice.
If we can fool him one more time,
he'll never come back
to bother us again.
But he'll be mighty hard to fool
the third time."

Wiley's mother sat down
in her rocking chair
and she thought.

Wiley couldn't sit still.

He went outside

and tied up one dog

at the front door.

He tied up the other dog

at the back door.

Then he came inside.

He crossed a broom and an ax

over the window.

He built a fire in the fireplace.

Then he sat down

and helped his mother think.

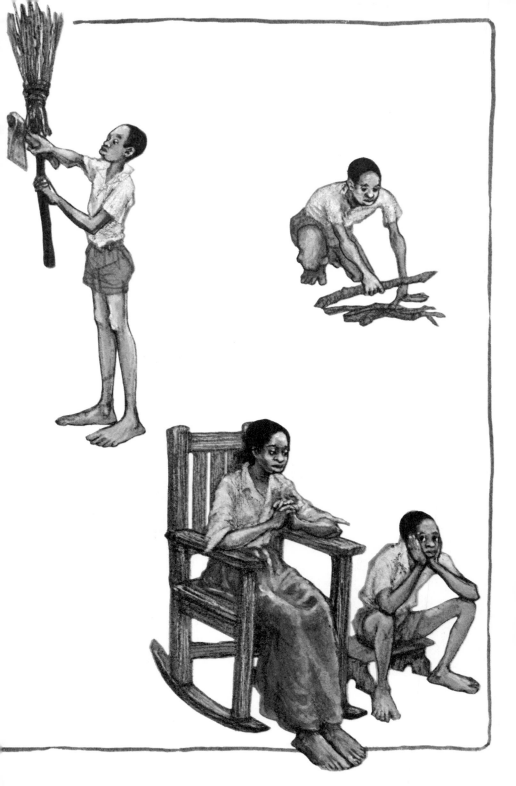

After a while she said,
"Wiley, go down to the pen
and bring me back a young pig."
Wiley went down to the pen
and brought her back a piglet.
She put the piglet in Wiley's bed.

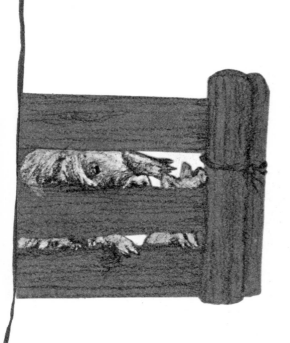

His mother said,
"Wiley, you go up
to the loft and hide."
Wiley climbed up
to the loft.

He looked out front

through a knothole in a plank.

He saw a great big animal

run out of the swamp toward the house.

The dog out front broke loose.

It chased the animal

back into the swamp.

Wiley looked out back through
a crack between the planks.
He saw another animal run out of
the swamp toward the house.
The other dog broke loose.
It chased the animal
back into the swamp.

The wind howled and the house shook.
Wiley heard footsteps on the roof
over his head. It was the Hairy Man.
He was trying to come down
the chimney. When the Hairy Man
touched the chimney and found
it was hot, he cursed and swore.
Then he jumped down from the roof,
and he walked right up to the front door.
He banged on it and yelled out,
"Momma, I've come for your young'un!"
But Wiley's mother called back,
"You can't have him, Hairy Man!"

The Hairy Man said,
"I'll set your house on fire with lightning.
I'll burn it down
if you don't give him to me!"

But Wiley's mother called back,
"I have plenty of
sweet milk, Hairy Man.
The milk will
put out your fire."

Then the Hairy Man said,
"I'll dry up your cow.
I'll dry up your spring.
I'll send a million boll weevils
out of the ground
to eat up your cotton
if you don't give me your young'un."
"Hairy Man," said Wiley's mother,
"you wouldn't do all that.
That's mighty mean."
"I'm a mighty mean man,"
said the Hairy Man.

So Wiley's mother said,
"If I do give you the young'un,
will you go away
and never come back?"
"I swear I will," said
the Hairy Man.

Wiley's mother opened the door.

"He's over in that bed," she said.

The Hairy Man grinned and grinned.

He walked over to the bed.

He snatched the covers back.

"Hey!" he yelled.
"There's nothing in this bed
but a young pig!"
"I never said which young'un
I'd give you,"
Wiley's mother answered.
The Hairy Man stomped his feet.
He gnashed his teeth.
He raged and yelled.

Then he grabbed the piglet
and fled away with it into the swamp.

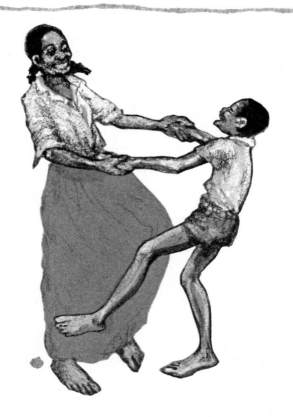

Wiley came down from the loft.

"Is the Hairy Man gone for good?"

"He sure is," said Wiley's mother.

"He can't ever get you now."

Wiley and his mother had fooled
the Hairy Man three times,
and they never saw him again.

"But if you didn't get the part," said Brother, "why are you smiling?"

"Because I've got good news about another part," said Bonnie. "Bearamount Pictures has withdrawn its offer to Shirley Bruin. She won't be playing the part of Rose O'Beara after all."

"That hardly sounds like good news," said Ferdy. "It sounds more like a major setback. It could hold up shooting for a long time."

"Not so," said Bonnie. "Because they've already found someone else to play Rose O'Beara."

"They have?" said Brother. "Who?"

Bonnie's smile broadened into a dreamy grin. "You're lookin' at her," she said.

BIG CHAPTER BOOKS

The Berenstain Bears and the Drug Free Zone
The Berenstain Bears and the New Girl in Town
The Berenstain Bears Gotta Dance!
The Berenstain Bears and the Nerdy Nephew
The Berenstain Bears Accept No Substitutes
The Berenstain Bears and the Female Fullback
The Berenstain Bears and the Red-Handed Thief
The Berenstain Bears
    and the Wheelchair Commando
The Berenstain Bears and the School Scandal Sheet
The Berenstain Bears and the Galloping Ghost
The Berenstain Bears at Camp Crush
The Berenstain Bears and the Giddy Grandma
The Berenstain Bears and the Dress Code
The Berenstain Bears' Media Madness
The Berenstain Bears in the Freaky Funhouse
The Berenstain Bears
    and the Showdown at Chainsaw Gap
The Berenstain Bears in Maniac Mansion
The Berenstain Bears at the Teen Rock Cafe
The Berenstain Bears and the Bermuda Triangle
The Berenstain Bears
    and the Ghost of the Auto Graveyard
The Berenstain Bears and the Haunted Hayride
The Berenstain Bears and Queenie's Crazy Crush
The Berenstain Bears and the Big Date
The Berenstain Bears and the Love Match
The Berenstain Bears and the Perfect Crime (Almost)
The Berenstain Bears Go Platinum
The Berenstain Bears and the G-Rex Bones
The Berenstain Bears Lost in Cyberspace
The Berenstain Bears in the Wax Museum
The Berenstain Bears Go Hollywood

The Berenstain Bears

by the Berenstains

A BIG CHAPTER BOOK™

Random House 🏠 New York

www.randomhouse.com/kids
www.berenstainbears.com

Library of Congress Cataloging-in-Publication Data
Berenstain, Stan, 1923–
The Berenstain Bears go Hollywood / by the Berenstains.
    p. cm. — (A big chapter book)
SUMMARY: The Bearamount Pictures studio has a huge effect on Beartown
when it comes to shoot the new movie "Lost with the Wind" and Bonnie is
chosen to play a principal role.
ISBN 0-679-88948-5 (trade) — ISBN 0-679-98948-X (lib. bdg.)
[1. Motion pictures—Production and direction—Fiction.
2. Bears—Fiction.]   I. Berenstain, Jan, 1923– . II. Title.
III. Series: Berenstain, Stan, 1923– . Big chapter book.
PZ7.B4483Bemkj   1999
[Fic]—dc21
99-24466

Printed in the United States of America   10 9 8 7 6 5 4 3 2 1

RANDOM HOUSE and colophon are registered trademarks of Random
House, Inc. BIG CHAPTER BOOKS and colophon are trademarks of
Berenstain Enterprises, Inc.

Contents

Chapter 1
The Three-Camera Stranger

By Bear Country standards, Big Bear City was a metropolis. It had four motels and two big hotels—and that was just within the city limits. It had lots of office buildings, dozens of eating places, three newspapers, a big-time TV station, and a large population. It was the sort of place where strangers were hardly noticed.

But Beartown was a very different sort of place. It had only one motel and a single office building. There were a number of businesses (at least half of which were owned by multimillionaire Squire Grizzly), but only one newspaper and a small population, even when you counted the folks who lived outside the town limits. Beartown was the sort of place where a stranger stuck out like a thumb with a big bandage on it.

And that's exactly how the stranger who checked into the Grizzly Arms Motel one day stuck out. He would have aroused curiosity even if he hadn't taken three cameras wherever he went—a big one that hung from a shoulder strap and two smaller ones that hung from his neck. He would have been noticed even if he hadn't gone around taking pictures of just about everything in sight. There didn't seem to be much of a pattern to what he snapped. He snapped everything from the statue of General Bearegard in the town square to the historic courthouse where Judge Gavel presided.

Judge Gavel was too busy studying court papers to look out his office window long enough to notice the stranger. But he found

out about him as soon as Burt McBurt, the
court reporter, knocked on his office door
and peeked in.

"Sorry to bother you, Your Honor," said
Burt. "It's important."

"Well, don't just stand there with your
head pokin' through the door," said Judge
Gavel.

Burt stepped into the room and gestured
at the window. "There's a stranger out there

takin' pictures of the courthouse."

"And?"

"Well, what d'ya suppose he's up to, Judge?"

"How am I supposed to know?" said Judge Gavel. "If you're so curious, why don't you ask him?"

"I tried that," said Burt. "But when I went up to him on the courthouse steps, he turned around and took a picture of *me!* Can he do that, Judge? Isn't that an invasion of privacy or something?"

Judge Gavel sighed. "You have no right to privacy on the courthouse steps, Burt," he said. "It's a public place."

"There oughta be a law," Burt complained.

"Well, there isn't," said the judge. "Now will you please get out of here so I can take my nap?"

Burt left, and Judge Gavel went to the window to pull down the shade. Sure enough, there was the stranger out in the town square. He was taking a picture of Old Shag, the historic shagbark hickory in whose shade Generals Stonewall Grizzly and Ulysses S. Bear signed the treaty to end the Great Bear War.

"Hmm," said the judge to himself. "Probably a tourist." Then he stretched out on the office couch and within seconds was sound asleep.

Quite a few Beartown folks who noticed the stranger had the same thought as Judge Gavel about what the fellow was doing in Beartown. But there were other ideas, too. Earlier that day, right after the stranger had checked into the Grizzly Arms Motel, the desk clerk had turned to the maid cleaning the office and said, "He's obviously a sites guy."

"What's a sites guy?" asked the maid.

"A guy sent somewhere by a company to find a good place to build a factory or warehouse."

Later that day, too, more guesses were made when the stranger ventured beyond the city limits. At one point, Sister Bear saw him and said to Papa, "There's a guy outside taking pictures of our house."

Papa went to the window. "Hmm," he said. "Wonder what he's up to."

"Oh, my!" said Mama, joining Papa. "I'll bet he's from *Tree House Beautiful* and he's going to put our house in the magazine!"

"That'd be cool," said Brother.

"I'd better go find out," said Papa. "Oh, sir!" he called from the front steps. "Are you from *Tree House Beautiful?*"

The stranger looked up and said, "What? Oh, yes, indeed—your tree house certainly is beautiful." Then he did what he usually did when someone asked him what he was up to. He took Papa's picture. And hopped into his rental car and drove off.

Chapter 2
Cut Me In

The next morning, Ralph Ripoff was having breakfast at the Red Berry when he saw the stranger out on the sidewalk, taking a snapshot of the restaurant. Ralph was Beartown's resident small-time swindler and conbear, and he was very protective of his turf. Whenever he saw a stranger who appeared to be checking Beartown out, he automatically assumed it was another crook up to some sort of mischief. His first instinct was usually to chase the intruder away. But in this case he had a different reaction.

Hmm, thought Ralph. *That young fellow is willing to risk being noticed walking around and snapping pictures in broad daylight. He must be playing for pretty high stakes...*

Just then, the stranger turned to snap a picture of Great Grizzly National Bank across the street.

Aha! thought Ralph. *So that's his game! Casing the bank. Maybe I can get in on this...*

Ralph threw some bills down on the table and hurried outside. "Hi there, stranger!" he said. "Ripoff's the name, swindling's the game. And I know exactly what you're up to."

The stranger, who had been about to take Ralph's picture, lowered his camera and frowned. "You do?" he said.

"Sure," said Ralph. "It's as plain as the

nose on your face. And if you want me to keep quiet about it, you're gonna have to cut me in."

"Cut you in?" said the stranger. "Oh, I see." He sighed. "Well, I *would* like to keep it a secret for another day or two—"

"Ah, so the job's gonna be soon, is it?" said Ralph.

"Huh?" said the stranger.

"Let's walk while we talk," said Ralph. "In

our business, it helps to keep moving."

As they strolled off down the street, Ralph continued, "I'll tell you what, my friend. For five hundred dollars, I'll keep quiet. But for a thousand, I'll lend you a helping hand. What'll it be?"

"Actually," said the stranger, "I could use some help identifying the Beartown folks whose pictures I've taken."

"My goodness!" said Ralph. "You boys sure know how to prepare for a job! Identifying potential witnesses before the crime so you can threaten them later—very impressive!"

"Witnesses?" said the stranger. "Crime? What are you talking about?"

"You don't have to be coy with me, young fella," Ralph chuckled. "Like I said: I already know you're planning to rob Great Grizzly National Bank."

The stranger stopped in his tracks. He looked shocked. Then he threw his head back and laughed.

"Stop that!" snapped Ralph. "You're attracting attention!"

"But you've got me all wrong, Mr. Ripoff," said the stranger. He offered his hand. "Name's Jake. I work for Bearamount Pictures in Hollywood. I've been sent out here by the great movie director Cecil Bear

STOP THAT! YOU'RE ATTRACTING ATTENTION!

DeMille to scout a location for his up-coming epic movie of the best-selling novel *Lost with the Wind*."

Ralph's eyes grew wide. "Bearamount Pictures?" he said. "Cecil Bear DeMille? *Lost with the Wind?* Are you putting me on, son?"

"No," said Jake. "After all, *Lost with the Wind* is about the Great Bear War. And in those days, Beartown was right in the mid-dle of the action. The Battle of Beartown was the final battle of the war, the one that led the Grizzly clan to surrender to the Bear clan. Where better to shoot the movie than Beartown?"

"Agreed," said Ralph. "But why take pictures of modern buildings like the bank and the restaurant? You can't use those in a historical movie."

"Sure we can," said Jake. "Our set designer needs pictures of them so he'll know how to fix them up to look old-fashioned."

"But why do you need pictures of Beartown folks?" asked Ralph.

"For casting purposes," said Jake. He glanced quickly around to make sure no one else was within earshot. "You see, C.B.—that's Mr. DeMille—likes to cast locals in his movies whenever he's on location. In

Lost with the Wind, only the main characters will be played by real actors. All the other roles will be filled by ordinary Beartown citizens."

"Oh, I see," said Ralph. "That's why you want to keep it a secret for a while."

"At least until we're all set up for auditions," said Jake. "If word got out too soon, I'd be mobbed by Beartown folks who wanted to get their faces onto the silver screen. Now, let's get these pictures identified."

"I've got the perfect place for working unobserved," said Ralph. "Ralph's Place, my secluded houseboat on the lovely banks of Old Grizzly River."

"Lead the way," said Jake.

And off they went.

Chapter 3
You Ought to Be in Pictures

A couple of days later, Bearamount Pictures informed the Beartown media of its plan to shoot *Lost with the Wind* in and around Beartown. Instantly, TV and radio were full of the news. BEARTOWN GOES HOLLYWOOD!! screamed the *Beartown Gazette*'s lead headline. AUDITIONS FOR *LOST WITH THE WIND* START TODAY!

With Bear Country School closed for the summer, Bearamount Pictures and town officials had agreed to hold auditions in the school auditorium. Some Beartown folks—the ones who looked right for particular roles—were actually invited to audition. Tops on this list was Ralph Ripoff, who seemed perfect for the role of Sam Sleaze, a

double spy who worked for both sides in the war between the blue-uniformed Bear clan and the gray-uniformed Grizzly clan. With his old-fashioned straw hat, spats, and walking stick, Ralph wouldn't even need a costume! Next on the list was Squire Grizzly, Beartown's multimillionaire businessbear. Ralph had told Jake that the squire was a

direct descendant of General Stonewall Grizzly, who led the Gray troops into the fateful Battle of Beartown. Cecil Bear DeMille decided it would be a great gimmick to have the small part of Stonewall Grizzly played by a direct descendant of the great general. Ditto with Papa Q. Bear, a direct descendant of General Ulysses S. Bear, who defeated Stonewall Grizzly at the Battle of Beartown.

Ralph, Papa, and the squire all read well in their auditions, so they got the parts. That left Mayor Horace J. Honeypot the part of mayor of Beartown during the Great Bear War. The only trouble was his reading. To say it wasn't very good would be an understatement. And to say it was a disaster wouldn't be an exaggeration. The mayor was famous for mixing up his words, and when he was asked to read the line "We must put a stop to this terrible war!" he read it as "We must soot a pop to this wurrible tore!" They gave him a second chance, but "On the graves of my ancestors, I vow never to give up!" came out as "On the ants of my gravecestors, I now leave her to give up!" Finally, the casting crew decided to give the mayor the part anyway but dub his lines with a real actor's voice.

After the invitees, the general public auditioned. The crush of folks in the schoolyard lessened as a few bears at a time were led into the auditorium and put through their paces. Of course, folks knew that the parts they'd be cast in were small—mostly nonspeaking parts that weren't much to speak of, so to speak. The famous actor Clark Grizzle had been cast as the male lead, Rett Cutler, and the famous actress Vivian Brie had been cast opposite him as Scarlett O'Beara. All the other major roles as well had been filled by professional actors and actresses. Except, that is, for the role of Scarlett's younger sister, Rose. Bearamount was still haggling with the well-known cub actress Shirley Bruin over the terms of a contract for that role.

Casting for the small parts went at a rapid pace. Biff Bruin, owner of Biff Bruin's

Pharmacy, was cast as the proprietor of the Beartown General Store, and Chief Bruno, Beartown's police chief, was cast as—you guessed it—Beartown's police chief. Teacher Bob filled the role of the town doctor, and Dr. Gert Grizzly, after much grumbling, accepted the role of his nurse. Other adult roles were filled by Bear Country School staff: Teacher Jane, Principal Honeycomb, Mr. Grizzmeyer, and Miss Glitch.

Then things hit a snag. The casting crew wanted to put Farmer Ben in the role of General Stonewall Grizzly's personal attendant and Two-Ton Grizzly in the role of

General Ulysses S. Bear's personal attendant. But Farmer Ben refused. He said the Bens were members of the Bear clan and it wouldn't be right for a member of his clan to play the personal attendant of the enemy's general.

"Likewise," said Two-Ton Grizzly. "I'm a *Grizzly*—always have been and always will be. And I ain't gonna play no attendant to that Ulysses S. *Bear!*"

The astonished casting director looked

from one ornery bear to the other and scratched his head. "But, fellas," he said, "the Blue and Gray aren't enemies anymore. They made war over a hundred years ago. And then they made *peace*."

"Don't matter," insisted Farmer Ben. "That's just the way I feel."

Two-Ton didn't even have to say anything. From the way he folded his powerful arms across his massive chest and frowned at the casting director, it was pretty clear he felt the same way Farmer Ben did.

"Well, why don't we just switch your roles?" suggested the casting director. "Farmer Ben, you play General Bear's attendant. And, Two-Ton, you play General Grizzly's. How's that?"

Farmer Ben's face broke into a broad smile. "Why, I'd be honored," he said.

Two-Ton grinned from ear to ear. "It'd be a privilege," he said.

And that settled that. At least, for the time being.

Competition for cub roles was intense. That's because there were only two of them: a drummer boy for the Blue army, and a girlfriend of Rose O'Beara's. Brother Bear had started drum lessons earlier in the summer, and he hoped his drumming skill would land him the first role. His best friend, Bonnie Brown, was the odds-on favorite to get the role of Rose's girlfriend, since she had done some professional acting in TV commercials.

For his audition, Brother was ordered to march across the stage while pretending to play a snare drum. It was a cinch. He was told right then and there that he had the part, and he strutted out to the schoolyard to bask in the admiration of his friends and wait for Bonnie to finish her audition. As he

waited, he thought fondly of what lay ahead. Wouldn't it be great to be on a big Hollywood movie set with Bonnie? Neither of them would have much to do, so they could pass the time just hangin' out as the whole glamorous Hollywood thing unfolded right before their eyes!

"I'll bet Bonnie gets that part," said Babs Bruno.

"Of course she'll get it," said Brother. "Who else?"

"I might remind you," said Ferdy Factual, "that Queenie McBear is also auditioning for that role."

"Oh, please!" scoffed Brother. "Queenie? I'll admit she's been okay in school plays, but against Bonnie she doesn't stand a chance."

"Shh!" said Sister Bear. "Here comes Bonnie."

Bonnie strolled up to the group. She was smiling.

"So," said Brother, "who got the role of Rose O'Beara's friend? *As if I didn't know.*"

"Queenie," said Bonnie matter-of-factly. "At least, I assume she'll get it. Because I didn't."

The group let out a gasp. "You didn't?" said Brother. "Are you pulling my leg?"

"I'm not even touching you," said Bonnie, still smiling.

"But if you didn't get the part," said Brother, "why are you smiling?"

"Because I've got good news about another part," said Bonnie. "Bearamount Pictures has withdrawn its offer to Shirley Bruin. She won't be playing the part of Rose O'Beara after all."

"That hardly sounds like good news," said Ferdy. "It sounds more like a major setback.

It could hold up shooting for a long time."

"Not so," said Bonnie. "Because they've already found someone else to play Rose O'Beara."

"They have?" said Brother. "Who?"

Bonnie's smile broadened into a dreamy grin. "You're lookin' at her," she said.

Chapter 4
Hotline to Hollywood

It took a few seconds for what Bonnie had just told her friends to sink in. Then there were cries of "Wow!", "Cool!", and "Awesome!"

"That's fantastic!" said Brother. "How did it happen?"

"Well," said Bonnie, "I brought my own material for the audition: the balcony speech from Shakesbear's *Romeo and Juliet*. You know—'Romeo, oh, Romeo...wherefore art thou Romeo?' Anyway, they ate it up. Then the casting director recognized me from one of my TV commercials. And he called C.B. in Hollywood to get his okay to cast me as Rose O'Beara."

"C.B.?" said Brother.

"Cecil Bear DeMille," said Bonnie. "That's what everybody who knows him calls him."

"But you don't know him," Brother pointed out. "At least, not yet."

"Oh, but I do," said Bonnie. "I just talked to him on the phone."

"Awesome!" said Babs. "What did he say?"

"He said, 'They tell me you ought to be in pictures, kid,'" said Bonnie. "Then he asked me if I thought I could handle such a big role. I told him I could handle anything he threw at me—that I could even stand in for Vivian Brie if necessary. That made him laugh. I think he likes me! Just think, guys: working for *Cecil Bear DeMille,* the greatest

movie director of all time! This is my big break! I mean, TV commercials are fine, but *Lost with the Wind...!*"

Just then, Queenie came running up. "I got it!" she said. "I got the part!"

"Oh, really?" said Ferdy.

"No, O'Reilly," said Queenie. "Heather O'Reilly, Rose O'Beara's best friend."

"How exciting!" said Babs. "Hey, let's all go to the Burger Bear to celebrate. Milkshakes all 'round! I'm buying!"

Everyone nodded eagerly. Except Bonnie. "Oh, dear," she said. "I'd like to come, but I can't."

Brother gave her a disappointed look. "You mean you're gonna turn down a free milkshake?"

"Clark Grizzle and Vivian Brie are on their way from Hollywood right now," said Bonnie. "The casting director asked me if I'd like to go with him to meet their plane in Big Bear City. And, of course, I said yes!"

Queenie nearly crushed Bonnie with a hug. "You lucky girl!" she cooed. "Clark Grizzle and Vivian Brie!"

"Well, we could postpone the celebration until tonight," suggested Brother.

"Tonight?" said Bonnie. "Oh, no, I can't. Rehearsals start day after tomorrow, and I've got a ton of lines to learn."

"Tomorrow for lunch?" said Brother weakly.

"Tomorrow I'm having lunch with Clark, Vivian, and C.B.," said Bonnie. "C.B.'s flying in tomorrow morning, you know. Oh, I'd better go back in; I forgot to pick up my script! And we're leaving right away for the airport..." She hurried into the school without even saying good-bye.

Queenie gazed dreamily after Bonnie. "That girl's headed for stardom," she sighed. "And she's gonna leave the rest of us far, far behind..."

Chapter 5
Lights...Camera...Action!

Brother was upset at first about Bonnie ignoring him and her other friends. But he realized she had a really big role that would require a lot of work. He knew that down deep, she was the same old Bonnie who cared about her friends. And he was sure that when Saturday night came around, she would keep their regular weekly movie date. There would be no rehearsal or shoot on Sunday, so Bonnie wouldn't be so pressed for time to practice her lines on Saturday night.

Even if Brother hadn't calmed himself down about Bonnie, his disappointment might have been blown away by the sheer excitement of the first day of rehearsal. The first scene to be rehearsed was a love scene between Rett Cutler and Scarlett O'Beara. To be specific, it was a *kissing* scene—the most romantic scene in the movie, with a long, passionate kiss framed by a long, passionate close-up. That might seem a little odd, since kissing scenes rarely start movies. But, you see, movies aren't shot in sequence. All kinds of factors—money, weather, and actors' and actresses' health, just to name a few—determine the order in which scenes are shot. Later, the scenes are put into the right order by the director and the film editors.

Everyone assembled for the kissing scene. Cecil Bear DeMille, megaphone in hand and beret on head, was perched on the high director's chair with MR. DEMILLE printed across the back. Clark Grizzle and Vivian Brie were lounging in lower chairs that also had their names on them. A bunch of lighting, sound, and camera equipment and their operators surrounded and over-hung the small patch of ground at the edge of Birder's Woods where the scene was to take place. And surrounding all that were about a hundred Beartown folks who had come out to watch. Most of them were chattering excitedly.

Mr. DeMille raised his megaphone and boomed, "Quiet on the set!" Instantly, the

only sound left was the singing of birds in the nearby woods. When the greatest movie director in Bear Country spoke, you listened! Especially when he spoke through a megaphone.

"Players, take your places," said DeMille. Clark Grizzle and Vivian Brie moved to the center of the set.

It was at that point that Brother Bear, who was kneeling on the ground next to the camerabear, noticed an old orange crate on

the ground right next to Clark Grizzle. "Psst!" he said to the camerabear. "Someone forgot to clear the orange crate!"

"Don't worry, kid," the camerabear said over his shoulder. "It's for Mr. Grizzle to stand on while he's kissing Ms. Brie. Can't you see he's a full head shorter than she is? The whole scene is a close-up on their faces, so the crate won't show up in the movie."

Then the driver on the back of his motorized camera platform took it right up to the two actors. Clark Grizzle stepped up onto the orange crate and embraced Vivian Brie.

"Okay, Bill?" said DeMille.

"Ready when you are, C.B.," replied the camerabear.

The bear with the clacker jumped in front of the camera. "Scene thirty-eight, take one," he said, then clacked his clacker and stepped out of the camera's view.

"All right," said DeMille. "Lights…camera…action!"

Grizzle and Brie stared soulfully into each other's eyes. Their lips met. Then there was a loud CRACK! Suddenly, Grizzle was a full head shorter than Brie again.

"Cut!" cried DeMille.

It took a couple of seconds for the crowd to realize what had happened. Then they burst into laughter. Clark Grizzle was no longer standing on the orange crate. He was standing *in* the orange crate, whose top slats had cracked and given way under his feet.

"Get another crate!" barked DeMille. "And test it this time!"

"No more crates, C.B.," said a young bear who was running madly back and forth.

"Then get a chair, you idiot!" growled DeMille.

"Right away, C.B.!" said the prop bear, and disappeared into the crowd. He returned moments later with a wooden chair.

"Quiet on the set!" said DeMille. "Players, take your places."

Clark Grizzle mounted the chair and embraced Vivian Brie.

"Okay, Bill?" said DeMille.

"Ready when you are, C.B.," came the answer.

The clacker bear reappeared. "Scene thirty-eight, take two." *Clack!*

"All right," said the director. "Lights… camera…"

But before he could say, "Action!" the chair Grizzle was standing on collapsed, sending the actor head over heels. He landed smack on his face in the grass. The

crowd laughed hilariously as he stumbled to his feet, picking grass stems from between his teeth.

"You nincompoop!" yelled DeMille at the trembling prop bear. "That's a breakaway chair for the barroom brawl scene! Get a real chair! Pronto!"

But pronto wasn't quick enough. Clark Grizzle, scowling at the still laughing crowd, roared, "Shut up, you bunch of hicks!" and stomped off to his dressing room in a nearby trailer. And he didn't come out again for the rest of the day's shoot.

Chapter 6
You're the Greatest!

The great Cecil Bear DeMille had never lost a whole day's shoot in his life, and he wasn't about to start now—not with the biggest, most expensive movie he'd ever made. He was working with the tightest budget Bearamount Pictures had ever given him, so he had to put every minute of available shooting time to good use.

With Clark Grizzle sulking in his trailer all day, DeMille rearranged the shooting schedule. Instead of the kissing scene, he shot some scenes with Scarlett and Rose O'Beara. This involved moving the stars' trailers, including Bonnie's, because the scenes took place on the grounds of Grizzly Mansion. (Bonnie had her very own trailer with her name on it above a big gold star.)

Bonnie was great as Rose. In fact, she was far better prepared than Vivian Brie, who kept flubbing her lines. For one of the scenes, they needed fifteen takes to get it right!

At the end of the day, DeMille called Bonnie over. "You were terrific, kid," he told her. "A real trouper. I wish my grown-up actors were as good as you. Vivian muffing all those lines didn't even faze you."

"Thanks, C.B. I worked really hard

preparing. But what's going to happen with Clark? He was awfully upset."

"Oh, don't worry about him," said DeMille. "He storms off the set at least twice a week in every movie he makes. You just gotta know how to handle him. Watch this."

DeMille motioned the prop bear over. "Go to Mr. Grizzle's trailer," he said, "and tell him to get his furry behind back out here. I want to talk to him."

"Right away, C.B.," said the prop bear. He hurried off and did exactly what he'd been told to do. (Well, not *exactly;* he never mentioned Grizzle's "furry behind.")

After a while, Clark Grizzle, wearing a bathrobe and looking as if he were still smoldering inside, shuffled out to the set. "You wanted to see me, C.B.?" he muttered.

"You bet I do," said the director. "That thing you did with the chair, Clark! It was inspired! The best pratfall I've seen in all my directing days!"

"But...but it was an accident," said Grizzle.

"Who cares?" said DeMille. "It was fabulous! Better than W.C. Bruin! Better than Oliver Beary! Even better than Bearster Keaton! I'm telling you, Clark baby, it's time to make your move into comedy. I'm directing a slapstick comedy for my next movie, and I just might make you the star!"

Grizzle was smiling now. "No kidding, C.B.?" he said. "I've always wanted to act in a comedy."

"Who says you'll need to *act?*" DeMille said under his breath. Then, to Grizzle, he

said, "So, you'll be ready tomorrow morning for the kissing scene?"

"Ready when you are, C.B.!" said Clark brightly. He turned and headed for his trailer with a spring in his step.

"See," said DeMille to Bonnie. "You have to know how to treat these big stars. Stroke their egos. Deep down, most of them are just little cubs showin' off. By the way, the owner of the Bearjou Theater, Fred Furry, has invited me, Clark, and Vivian to a special movie screening Saturday night. Wanna tag along?"

"You bet!" said Bonnie. "What's the movie?"

"*The Bear Commandments,* starring Clark Grizzle and Vivian Brie, directed by yours truly," said DeMille. "Furry's gonna reserve the entire balcony for us. It's a nice little publicity stunt. It'll be good for us and great for Furry. It'll turn the Bearjou into a land-mark theater overnight—you know, 'C.B. DeMille slept here,' that kind of thing. I always fall asleep at movies. Anyway, I'll have my limousine pick you up at eight."

"Gee, thanks, C.B.," cooed Bonnie. "You're the greatest!"

The director smiled. "So they say," he replied.

GEE, THANKS, C.B. YOU'RE THE GREATEST!

Chapter 7
Not So Easy Rider

The great C.B. DeMille never planned out his rehearsal or shooting schedules too far in advance or in too great detail. That's because things depended too much on factors that were hard to predict, such as the weather, expenses, and whether or not one of his stars was sulking in his or her trailer.

Now DeMille decided to devote Friday and Saturday to the climax of *Lost with the Wind*: the Battle of Beartown, followed by the Gray's surrender to the Blue. The battle scene in particular was so complicated that a full two days of rehearsal were necessary. It involved hundreds of extras bused in from Big Bear City to play soldiers, and all of them, of course, had to be provided with uniforms and weapons. A dozen authentic Great Bear War cannons had been shipped to Beartown from national parks, museums, and Great Bear War cemeteries all over Bear Country. It was lucky that Miss Mamie's Riding Academy was located on the outskirts of Beartown, so Bearamount Pictures didn't have to bring cavalry horses in from out of town.

DeMille spent all day Friday mapping out the elaborate troop movements—charges, retreats, skirmishes, standoffs—that he hoped would make his Battle of Beartown the greatest battle scene in movie history. Then he had the extras on foot and horseback do a walk-through of the scene. On Saturday, he had them do the scene at full speed. They ran (and galloped), jumped, staggered, and fell. It took all day to get the extras who had been chosen to

fall in battle to act as if they were really getting shot or having shells explode at their feet. The special effects that would create the illusion of gunfire and explosions were so expensive that they had to be saved for the actual shooting.

Everything went surprisingly smoothly. Until Saturday afternoon, that is. The commanding officers of the Blue and the Gray were Papa Bear and Squire Grizzly, who had spent so much time on horses while growing up that he was bowlegged. But Papa had never been on a horse in his life. Rehearsal had to be stopped for two hours while Miss Mamie trained Papa to ride a trotting horse. (A galloping horse was out of the question for a beginner.)

On the very first attempt to have Papa lead his troops out of Birder's Woods and onto the battlefield, something completely unexpected happened. Cousin Fred's dog, Spot, who had been sitting calmly at the rear of the crowd, suddenly yanked his leash out of Fred's grasp and ran onto the battlefield. He ran right under the feet of Papa's horse, who whinnied and reared up on his hind legs, throwing his rider. Papa did a crazy flip and landed right on his head.

"Get that flea-bitten dog off my set!" roared DeMille. "Who's the owner?"

"Er...uh, th-that would be m-me, sir," said Fred sheepishly.

"You're out of the picture, kid!" shouted DeMille.

"B-but I'm not even *in* the picture," stammered Fred.

"No back talk!" snapped the director. "When I speak, you listen!"

Meanwhile, Miss Mamie rushed to grab her horse's reins. "Whoa, Diablo!" she said, then knelt at Papa's side. "Did he hurt you, Papa?"

Rubbing his neck, Papa propped himself up on an elbow and gave Miss Mamie a nasty look. "Hurt me?" he said. "How could you hurt anybody by throwing him on his head?"

Across the way, DeMille's assistant director was whispering in his ear. "That was a great pratfall, C.B.! Better than Clark's the other day. I think we should hire that guy for our next—"

"I don't pay you to think!" roared DeMille. "I pay you to make sure there aren't any *dogs on my set!*"

By now, the paramedics that DeMille kept on the set at all times were examining Papa. For the very first time in days of shooting, the great C.B. DeMille climbed down from his director's chair. He handed his megaphone to his assistant and walked out to where Papa was getting slowly to his feet. He talked briefly with the paramedics, then turned to Papa. "My medical boys say you're okay, Papa. Clean bill of health, won't even need a neck brace. Are you ready to proceed?"

"Well," said Papa, still rubbing his neck, "I guess what they say about getting right back on the horse comes into play here."

"No, no, that's not what I meant," said DeMille. "You get back on that horse and you'll just get yourself killed. I'll find a double to play you in the battle scene—you know, someone who looks enough like you that I can shoot him in profile and from a distance and nobody'll know it isn't you."

"Does that mean I'm out of the picture, C.B.?" moaned Papa.

"Of course not," said the director. "In fact, you and Squire Grizzly are gonna shoot the surrender scene right now. We're moving back to town."

"Can't we rehearse it first?" said Papa.

"No time," said DeMille. "We've got to hurry before that neck of yours stiffens up!"

Chapter 8
Surrender? Never!

The surrender scene was really quite simple. One camera would pan across the troops of the Blue and the Gray massed in the town square, then another camera would zoom in on Papa and Squire Grizzly standing under Old Shag, attended by Farmer Ben and Two-Ton Grizzly. The squire would draw his sword, say, "I hereby surrender the forces of the Grizzly clan to you, the commander of the Bear clan," and hand his sword to Papa. Papa would say, "As commander of the Bear clan's forces, I accept your surrender." Then the two would shake hands and be seated at a nearby table, where they would sign the peace treaty.

C.B. DeMille had never been told about the dispute earlier in the week over the roles played by Farmer Ben and Two-Ton Grizzly. As far as he was concerned, nothing could go wrong. Boy, was *he* in for a surprise!

"Quiet on the set!" boomed DeMille through his megaphone. "Actors, take your places!"

The clacker bear stepped in front of the camera. "Scene forty-two, take one." *Clack!*

"Okay, camerabears?" said DeMille.

"Ready when you are, C.B.," answered the two camerabears in unison.

"All right. Lights...camera...action!"

The scene went fine until Squire Grizzly opened his mouth to speak. "I hereby...," he said, then stopped. "I hereby...," he repeated.

"Cut!" said DeMille. "That's okay, Squire baby. Let's try it again. Just relax."

But take two didn't go any better. In fact, this time, when the squire opened his mouth to speak, Two-Ton Grizzly was heard to whisper, "Don't do it, Squire!"

"Cut!" cried DeMille. He scowled down at Two-Ton and the squire. "What the heck's goin' on here?"

Squire Grizzly was trembling with emotion. "I can't do it, C.B.," he said. "I can't

CUT!

bring myself to say the word 'surrender'!"

"You just said it!" growled DeMille.

"I mean I can't say it as General Grizzly," explained the squire. "It's bad enough that my great ancestor had to say it once. I would be dishonoring his sacred memory if I made him say it again after all these years. He'd turn over in his grave!"

"That's right!" said Two-Ton. "We're not gonna do it!"

"You?" sneered Farmer Ben. "It's not even your line, you big muscle-bound nitwit!"

Two-Ton made a threatening move toward Ben. "What did you call me, you old sack of fertilizer?"

The assistant director bravely jumped in between the two angry bears and did his best to keep them apart.

"ORDER ON THE SET!" screamed

DeMille at the top of his lungs.

Ben and Two-Ton stopped struggling with the assistant director. DeMille motioned them over. But instead of chewing them out, he looked warmly down at them and said, "I know this isn't easy for the two of you. But think about how your ancestors behaved at the end of the Battle of Beartown. Did they yell at each other? Did they fight? No. They behaved like the well-bred gentlebears they were. Now get back out there and behave like gentlebears. And send the squire over."

Squire Grizzly came over and stared defiantly up at the director.

"You say you don't want Stonewall Grizzly to turn over in his grave," said DeMille. "With all due respect, Squire, I submit to you that he is *already* turning over in his grave because of the way you're behaving. The great Stonewall Grizzly surrendered with grace and dignity, and I'm sure he'd want you to do the same. He'd want you to portray him just as he was, a great and honorable general in defeat even as in victory."

DeMille glanced at the sky. "We're losing the afternoon light," he said. "We'll reshoot this scene next week. In the meantime, Squire, I'd like you to think about what I've said."

As the squire walked away, Bonnie Brown hurried over to the director. "I'm so sorry, C.B.," she said. "I guess some Beartown folks are still a little testy about the Great Bear War."

"It's that big burly goon playing General Grizzly's attendant," muttered DeMille. "He's a troublemaker."

Bonnie rolled her eyes and laughed. "If you think *he's* bad," she said, "you should see his son, Too-Tall!"

Chapter 9
Stood Up

Immediately after the surrender scene fiasco, C.B. DeMille called a meeting with his crew and stars, including Bonnie. They gathered in his luxurious trailer, the inside of which looked like a four-star hotel room. He pulled no punches, telling them right off that he was already way over budget and that the whole project now depended on the success of Monday's shoot. The entire day would be devoted to shooting one scene: the Battle of Beartown, which was the trickiest and most expensive scene in the movie. If he failed to get a decent take, they would have to pack up, go back to

Hollywood, and forget all about *Lost with the Wind*.

"In the meantime," said the director, brightening, "it's Saturday night. Let's relax and have some fun. I'm taking you all out to dinner at the Red Berry before that publicity stunt at the Bearjou."

While the director, crew, and stars were heading to the Red Berry, Brother Bear was having dinner at home. He was really looking forward to his movie date with Bonnie and said so.

"Oh, yeah?" said Sister. "I hear she's gotten really stuck-up lately. She'll probably spend the whole movie jabbering about 'Clark' and 'Vivian' and 'C.B.'"

"Try to be a little tolerant, Sis," Brother scolded. "So she'll talk about the big stars she's been hanging out with. So what?"

"Well, I think you should call her," said

Sister. "Just to make sure the date's *still on*."

"Still on?" said Brother. "Of course it's still on! But I'd better give her a call anyway to make sure she wants me to pick her up at Grizzly Mansion like I usually do. She might be in some late movie conference and want to meet me at the Bearjou."

When Brother punched in the number for Grizzly Mansion in the family room, Lady Grizzly answered. "Oh, Bonnie?" she said. "She's not here, dear. I think she had to do something with C.B.—I mean, Mr.

DeMille. It's so difficult to keep up with her schedule now that she has a real Hollywood career, you know."

I was right, thought Brother as he hung up. She was on the set with DeMille, going over stuff for Monday. She was probably planning to meet him in line at the Bearjou.

It occurred to Brother that Bonnie might not have time to eat dinner, so he decided

to stop by the Burger Bear for takeout. Bonnie could eat during the movie. Surely Fred Furry would let her take food into the theater. After all, she was a big star now.

Brother got Bonnie a Grizzburger and fries at the Burger Bear and headed for the Bearjou. There was the usual Saturday night line to get tickets, but it wasn't the usual Saturday night length. It was about four times longer. It stretched down the sidewalk for two blocks. Brother saw Cousin Fred, Barry Bruin, and Babs Bruno near the middle of the line and went over. "I've never seen anything like this," he said.

"Yeah," said Fred. "Everybody got in line early because the balcony's reserved for the big shots. We're not all gonna get in, you know."

"I didn't think of that," said Brother. He looked up and down the line. "Seen Bonnie?"

"No, and I don't care to, either," said Fred. "She walked right past me on Grizzly Avenue yesterday and didn't even say hello."

"Maybe she didn't notice you," suggested Brother.

"No way," said Fred. "She just *pretended* she didn't notice me."

"The other day, I asked her to show me her dressing room," said Babs. "You know what she said? That she had to keep it 'clear' in case C.B. or Clark or Vivian stopped by. That girl's gone Hollywood big

time. I don't think I like her anymore."

Brother saw Queenie and Too-Tall farther up the line and went over. "Seen Bonnie?" he said.

"Wait'll you hear!" squealed Queenie. "Too-Tall just told me there's a rumor that Bonnie was invited to the movie by Cecil Bear DeMille. She's gonna sit in the balcony with DeMille, Clark Grizzle, and Vivian Brie!"

Brother's stomach did a backflip. "She is?" he mumbled. "But she was supposed to go to the movie with *me*..."

"Get over it, loser," said Too-Tall. "Bonnie's a big star now. There's a BNN van here. And Fred Furry even put out a red carpet for the stars to walk up."

BNN was the Bear News Network. Brother looked and saw the van parked at the curb down the street near the theater entrance. Just then, a camerabear and a reporter with a microphone got out and stood waiting on the sidewalk next to the red carpet.

"Hey, here come the stars!" said Queenie.

A silver stretch limousine glided up to the curb. The elegant chauffeur came around to open the rear curbside door. Out climbed the great Cecil Bear DeMille in his beret and smoking jacket, followed by Vivian Brie in an evening gown and Clark Grizzle in a black turtleneck and gray satin slacks. Last but not least—especially in

Brother's eyes—was Bonnie Brown. She was wearing a ton of brand-new jewelry and one of her coolest outfits, and her face was all aglow.

The BNN reporter hurried over to DeMille and started interviewing him. Brother waved and yelled, "Hey, Bonnie!"

But she didn't notice him. Or, rather, she *pretended* she didn't notice him.

Brother's heart sank—all the way down to his feet. He stared blankly at Bonnie, who was now being interviewed by the BNN reporter.

"Hey, come on," said Queenie. "The line's moving."

"Never mind," said Brother. "I don't even like this crummy movie anyway. Lousy acting. And even worse directing." Suddenly, he remembered the Grizzburger and fries he'd bought for Bonnie. In disgust, he looked down at the greasy bag in his hand, then casually tossed it into a nearby trash can.

"Two points," he muttered. And he headed home all alone.

Chapter 10
Acting Lesson

When Brother got home, he had no intention of calling Bonnie. He was too mad at her. And too hurt. But after passing the entire evening lying on his bed sulking, he decided it was high time to confront her. Someone had to tell her what she was doing. And who better to do it than her best friend?

Tillie, the maid, answered the phone at

Grizzly Mansion. "Oh, it's you, Master Brother," she said. "Bonnie isn't home yet. But wait...she just walked in the door..."

"What is it?" sighed Bonnie into the phone. "I'm *completely* exhausted..."

"What about our date tonight?" said Brother. "If you needed to cancel, you should have called me."

"I was meaning to call," said Bonnie, "but it was one thing after another, and I never had time. I thought you'd understand."

"I understand, all right," said Brother. "I understand that you're losing all your friends."

"What on earth are you talking about?" said Bonnie.

"Because of the way you've been acting lately," said Brother.

"I've been acting great!" said Bonnie. "C.B. said so himself!"

"That's not the kind of acting I meant—"
Brother started to say.

But Bonnie cut him off. "I really need to
go to bed now," she said, and hung up.

Brother stared at the phone for a while,
then hung up and sighed. "Well, that went
really well," he said to no one in particular.
Then he turned over and buried his face in
the pillow.

Chapter 11
Ready When You Are, C.B.!

As Sunday went and Monday came, Beartown was buzzing with questions. Had Bonnie Brown gone Hollywood to the point of damaging her hometown friendships beyond repair? Would Squire Grizzly be able to surrender to Papa Bear in their big scene—and, if so, would Two-Ton Grizzly be able to keep his big mouth shut? But the biggest question of all was: would Cecil Bear DeMille have to close up shop, go

back to Hollywood, and leave Beartown in the lurch? That, of course, depended on Monday's shoot of the Battle of Beartown.

As dawn broke, the armies of the Blue and the Gray assembled on the field called Buzzard Flats, next to Birder's Woods. Miss Mamie brought the cavalry horses in dozens of rented horse vans. Scores of explosive devices were carefully put in place by a team of special-effects experts. Sound equipment was scattered all over the vast set. Cameras were placed in various spots around the battlefield, in Birder's Woods, and across the highway. Bill, the head cam-erabear, would take aerial shots from a heli-copter hovering over the field.

This time, Cecil Bear DeMille had his megaphone in one hand and a walkie-talkie in the other.

"What's the walkie-talkie for?" Bonnie asked.

"So I can communicate with Bill up in the helicopter," said DeMille. "He's in direct contact with all the other camera-bears. After I cue him to roll 'em, he takes care of the rest. The only problem is, my walkie-talkie is on the fritz. It keeps cutting out."

"What'll you do?" asked Bonnie.

"Piece o' cake," said DeMille. "I told Bill I'd wave my arm back and forth three times to cue him to roll 'em."

Finally, everything was ready to go. The

dim morning sun would be backed up by huge floodlights all around the set. The director raised his megaphone. "Quiet on the set! Actors, take your places!"

Out popped the clacker bear. "Scene forty, take one!" *Clack!*

DeMille gazed out upon the vast scene and nodded. Bonnie heard him say, "Okay, this is it—do or die..."

"Lights!" he bellowed. Then he raised his right arm high above his head and waved it three times. "Action!"

For the next fifteen minutes, Birder's Woods and Buzzard Flats were mayhem. Troops charged back and forth, horses galloped to and fro, soldiers fell to earth, cannons fired, explosions filled the air with smoke and noise, horse-drawn wagons burst into flames.

Though DeMille had left the camera direction to Bill, he had to direct the special effects personally. The team of experts were clustered around his chair, clutching remote detonators. Through binoculars, the great director watched every little detail of the unfolding scene and at precisely the right moment barked, "Number one, now!", "Number two, now!", and so on, to cue the team to detonate their devices.

As the scene at last drew to a close, with a smoky haze enveloping the mock battle-field, it was obvious to crew and onlookers alike that the take had been a stunning suc-

cess. Then DeMille cried, "Cut! It's a wrap!" A huge ovation went up from the crowd. Whooping and hollering, crew members mobbed the great director, pumping his hand and slapping him on the back.

DeMille was beaming. His dream had come true. "We did it!" he yelled. "It's gonna be the greatest blockbuster of all time!"

Vivian Brie looked up at the sky. "Why doesn't Bill land the helicopter?" she asked.

"Probably waiting for the smoke to clear," said Clark Grizzle.

Just then, DeMille's walkie-talkie crackled. "Guess it's back on," he said, and lifted it to speak. "Everything okay up there, Bill?"

That's when the answer came back that twisted the director's grin into a grimace: "Ready when you are, C.B.!"

It was loud enough for the crew to overhear. Instantly, they went silent.

"What d'ya mean, 'ready'?" gasped DeMille. "D'ya mean you didn't shoot the scene?"

"Uh...er, no...," came the crackling reply. "I must have missed your cue. You see, I had a...uh, kind of a sneezing attack..."

DeMille didn't wait to hear the rest. "YOU'RE FIRED!" he screamed into the walkie-talkie. Then he threw it as hard as he could against the side of one of the horse vans. *Clang!*

"That's it," moaned the director. "We're finished! *Lost with the Wind* goes right into the garbage can!"

"What'll we tell the media, C.B.?" asked Vivian Brie.

DeMille clapped a hand against his forehead. "Oh, no!" he wailed. He could pic-

ture the newspaper headlines—things like
CAMERABEAR'S COLD DOOMS C.B. DEMILLE
EPIC! and THE SNEEZE HEARD 'ROUND THE
WORLD!

"Tell them whatever you want," muttered
DeMille. He turned to his assistant. "Call
Big Bear City and tell them to get my private jet ready. I'm flying back to Hollywood
tomorrow morning."

The director trudged off toward his limousine, but then he stopped and looked

back at the hovering helicopter one last time. That's when the helicopter finally moved. But it didn't land. Instead, it zoomed off and disappeared over Birder's Woods.

"Where's he going?" asked Vivian Brie.

Clark Grizzle gave a sneer and said, "As far as he can get on one tank of fuel."

Chapter 12
Lost with the Wind

By the next morning, the news had spread all over town. Everyone was in shock, especially the businessbears and shop owners who had expected *Lost with the Wind* to put Beartown on the map and bring in tourists and other business. Mayor Honeypot had already ordered a huge billboard for the road into Beartown, reading: BEARTOWN—HOME OF <u>LOST WITH THE WIND</u>. Now the order would have to be canceled. Unless, of course, the billboard was changed to BEARTOWN—HOME OF THE GREATEST FIASCO IN MOVIEMAKING HISTORY.

But of all the folks in Beartown, no one was more upset than Brother Bear. He was upset about the same things everyone else was: not getting to see himself on the silver screen and not getting to see Beartown become a household word all over Bear Country. But for Brother, those things were made even worse by the fact that Beartown's going Hollywood had also lost him his best friend.

So it was hardly surprising that by afternoon, Brother had sought out the place he always went when he was really upset—the spot he called his Thinking Place, a little clearing in the woods behind Bear Country School. It was quiet there. There were no sounds except the chirp of birds and the buzz of bees. It was a good place to gather your thoughts and mull things over in your mind.

Brother sat on his favorite rock and put his elbows on his knees and his head between his hands. Usually when he suffered some setback or disappointment, there was a lesson to be learned from it, something positive he could take away. But this time, it didn't seem like that at all. What was the lesson to be learned from the great movie fiasco? Stay away from Hollywood types? It's a bear-eat-bear world?

Somehow those lessons didn't seem very positive.

And then, all of a sudden, it hit him. He had spent so much time thinking about Bonnie's obnoxious behavior from his own point of view that he hadn't bothered to think of it from her point of view. That is to say, how would he have behaved if he'd been in Bonnie's place? It was hard to say. Maybe he would have behaved better. But maybe not. Maybe he would have been every bit as swept up in the glamour of a big Hollywood movie role. There really wasn't any way to know until it happened to you.

That made Brother realize that he shouldn't judge Bonnie too harshly. What was the old saying? Bears who live in glass houses shouldn't throw stones? As soon as he realized he wasn't so different from Bon-

nie, he felt closer to her again. And that made him feel better.

But then his heart sank again. There was a catch. Maybe his friendship with Bonnie really *was* damaged beyond repair...

Just then, he heard someone say, "Brother?" It was Bonnie, emerging from the woods behind him.

"Bonnie?" he said. "What are you doing here?"

"Oh, good," sighed Bonnie. "I thought you might not even be speaking to me."

"Because of Saturday night?" said Brother. "Oh, that's okay. I've been doing some thinking—"

"And so have I," said Bonnie, cutting him off. "And it's *not* okay. What you said about the way I've been acting lately...well, you were right. And I'm glad you told me, because it made me realize something. It's not important whether or not you're a big shot; what's important is how you treat other bears."

Brother smiled and put an arm around Bonnie. "I couldn't have said it better myself," he said. "And you know what? I might have gone Hollywood just as bad as you did if I'd gotten a big role in that movie. And if I had, I hope I'd have had the guts to admit it the way you just did."

"Thanks," said Bonnie. "But I'm afraid my other friends won't be so understanding."

"They will if you apologize to them," said Brother. "But let me talk to them first, tell them what you just told me. They'll take your apology better if I soften 'em up a little first."

Bonnie's face broke into a big grin. "Brother Bear," she said, "you're just about the best friend a best friend ever had."

The two cubs sat in silence for a while,

feeling good about each other again. A summer breeze was rising. They watched it rustle the leaves of the trees.

Finally, Brother said, "So what happens to your Hollywood career now?"

Just as the breeze was gusting, Bonnie shrugged and said, "Nothing, I guess. I got lost with the wind."

They had a good laugh at that.

Chapter 13
Back on the Breeze

But as things turned out, Bonnie was wrong about her Hollywood career. For as Cecil Bear DeMille was boarding his private jet in Big Bear City, he got a phone call that sent him rushing back to Beartown to resume shooting *Lost with the Wind.*

The call was from Squire Grizzly. He had thought long and hard about what the great director had told him on Saturday. And he had come to the decision that not only would he honor his famous ancestor Stonewall Grizzly by doing the surrender scene with grace and dignity, but that in order to so honor him, *Lost with the Wind* had to be made at any cost. And that's why, when he phoned C.B. DeMille at the airport, he pledged quite a few of his many millions to ensure that the epic movie would be completed.

When *Lost with the Wind* was finally done, Bearamount Pictures came up with a great publicity stunt. They flew the entire Beartown cast to Hollywood for the grand opening at the world-famous "Bearr" Theater. And this time, as the media's cameras rolled and their flashbulbs flashed, Bonnie Brown didn't walk up the red carpet from her limo on the arm of Cecil Bear DeMille

or Clark Grizzle or Vivian Brie. She walked up that red carpet hand in hand with her fellow cub actors, Brother Bear and Queenie McBear.

Perhaps the ovation wasn't as great as it might have been if she'd arrived with the big shots. But she felt good about it just the same.

And so did all her friends.

Stan and Jan Berenstain began writing and illustrating books for children in the early 1960s, when their two young sons were beginning to read. That marked the start of the best-selling Berenstain Bears series. Now, with more than one hundred books in print, videos, television shows, and even Berenstain Bears attractions at major amusement parks, it's hard to tell where the Bears end and the Berenstains begin!

Stan and Jan make their home in Bucks County, Pennsylvania, near their sons—Leo, a writer, and Michael, an illustrator—who are helping them with Big Chapter Books stories and pictures. They plan on writing and illustrating many more books for children, especially for their four grandchildren, who keep them well in touch with the kids of today.